Joy

The Next Chapter

By Kimberly Kirby

DEDICATION

Dedicated to all who have supported my dream by listening, reading, critiquing my work, or purchasing my stories. You have my eternal love and gratitude.

From my heart to yours,

Kimberly Kirby

CHAPTER 1

Sunlight spills into Angela's bedroom waking her from her sleep. She groggily looks at the other side of her bed; the covers are still neatly in place, the pillows still fluffed perfectly - David never came home last night.

Angela rolls over, covers her head with the blanket, and goes back to sleep.

It's been a year since David moved in and Angela can always tell when he has a new girlfriend. That's when he becomes the invisible man. Sometimes he disappears for days at a time without a word. Then, as if he's only been gone an hour, he stumbles in the front door, gives Angela a kiss and heads upstairs.

So far, it's been two days since she last saw him. At this point, it doesn't even hurt anymore. There's a numbness that comes over you after a while. You spend so much time trying to fool everyone into thinking that you're happy and "it's ok," that a small part of you starts to believe it.

An hour later the buzz of her cell phone, on the night stand, snaps her back into consciousness. It's Jonathan.

"Hello?" Angela mumbles, half asleep.

"Ma? I know you're not still in bed!" Jonathan laughs.

"I thought you were coming to church with us?"

"Oh, yea I forgot. I'm getting up now. I'll meet y'all at the church."

Angela hangs up the phone and runs to the bathroom to take a shower.

When she comes out she sees David, sitting on the edge of the bed taking off his shoes.

"Hey baby," he says as if nothing's wrong.

"Hey," Angela says with no emotion.

She makes her way over to the closet struggling to cover her nakedness with a red towel that's a bit too small.

She manages to make it into the large, walk in closet, without making eye contact with him. She can't bear to look him in the eye these days. Besides, that's normally what got her into trouble with him. He always had a way of looking in her eyes and making her feel safe and comfortable . . . right before he'd go out and screw some other woman.

Angela slides into a black pantsuit, her favorite red heels, and digs around for her red bag.

"Where you goin'?" David asks.

"Church," Angela answers plainly.

David lets out a dismissive chuckle.

"Yea, well make me some eggs before you go."

Angela walks out of the closet fully dressed bag in hand.

"Sure," she says with a sigh as she makes her way out of the bedroom, still not looking at him.

Angela speeds into the parking lot of Life Overcomers Church; she started coming here about eight months ago with Jonathan.

Now that he's in college and working a full time job, Sunday has really become their day to catch up and spend time together. Jonathan moved out about six months ago.

As heartbroken as Angela was, she knew it was the right decision for him. He grew tired of watching his mother be disrespected by David and the arguments between them were going from verbal to physical.

Walking into the church, Angela spots Jonathan sitting with Joy in the back row; she quickly ducks in and joins them. The pastor is already up preaching.

Pastor Johns is a handsome, brown skinned man with his hair cut very close to his head. He has the kind of eloquence that draws people in when they hear him speak. Since he's taken over, the church has tripled in size.

He has an over the top yet friendly personality. If he weren't the pastor you'd probably find yourself at a basketball game with him.

As always, Pastor Johns delivers a spirited sermon. Angela, Jonathan and Joy head out into the lobby. As Angela makes her way out of the door, she loses her footing, in her favorite pencil thin heels, and goes flying into the back of the man in front of her - almost knocking him down.

Jonathan grabs his mom and helps her regain her balance.

"Whoa, ma you ok?" Jon asks, still holding her up.

The man turns around, grabs Angela by the hand, and helps to steady her.

"It wasn't that bad was it?" The man asks.

"What?" Angela asks, shrinking in her embarrassment.

"The sermon? Pastor got you running out the building, huh?" The man lets out a loud boisterous laugh.

"Oh, no I . . . was just . . . um," Angela stammers.

"I'm just playing with you sista, you, ok?"

"Yea, I'm fine, sorry about that." Angela smiles suddenly noticing how handsome the stranger is.

"No need to apologize, I'm Will." He says shaking her hand.

Will is a handsome, dark skinned man of about forty years old. He's around 5'10 with a thick physique. You can tell he works out, but not overly so. He has broad shoulders, muscular arms, and a sly sexy smile with pretty white teeth.

"And you are?" He asks with a smile.

"Angela," she answers, realizing she's still holding his hand. She quickly drops it and steps back toward Jonathan.

"And, this is my son, Jonathan, and his girlfriend, Joy." Angela pushes Jon toward Will.

"This grown man is your son?" Will laughs as he shakes Jonathan's hand.

"Nice to meet y'all. Look, I'm 'bout to go get something to eat, you wanna join me?" Will asks the group but his eyes are intently focused on Angela.

"Sounds good to me, I'm hungry . . ." Jonathan starts eagerly but Angela quickly pinches him to shut him up.

"Jon, remember you have to take me to the store." Angela quickly blurts out.

"Oh, well that's okay. Maybe next Sunday." Will says, his kind eyes still fixated on Angela.

Will walks away, shaking hands and hugging other smiling church goers on his way out.

Joy is in her perfectly organized room busily doing her homework. Posted around the room are several pictures of her and Jonathan, almost too many. Every time she's around that boy she finds a reason to snap a picture with her cell phone.

Over the last year, her and Jon have graduated from high school and have excitedly begun their first year of college, at the University of Memphis. Joy has been coasting by easily, with her full scholarship and generous support from her parents.

Jon, on the other hand, is working a full time job to pay for his education and keep his apartment so he won't have to move back in with his mom and David.

As Joy works at her desk, her eyes start to wander about the room; she smiles at the pictures of her and Jon. Her gaze eventually settles on the bridal magazine sitting on her desk. She drops her pen, quickly grabs the magazine, and leafs through it. The pages are dog eared to her favorite wedding gowns.

Jonathan, despite his nagging doubts, is still engaged to Joy and she has been happily planning their wedding even though she can't get him to decide on a wedding date.

At that moment, Carla knocks on the door and quickly pokes her head in without waiting for a response.

"Dinner's ready, you coming down?" Carla leans in smiling.

"Yea, I'll be down in a minute." Joy replies warmly, turning her gaze back to her magazine.

It's funny . . . Joy and Carla never could seem to get along. Joy always felt that her mother never truly wanted her. She felt that her very existence was somehow a nuisance to Carla. She never felt love at home, only loneliness and uncertainty.

After Carla pushed Joy down the stairs, a change took place in their relationship. To Joy, that has been the one (and possibly the only) time Carla did anything to show how much she loved her. Until then Joy felt that Carla might love the woman that does her bi-weekly pedicure, with that perfect shade of baby pink, more than she loved her.

To Joy, it was a start.

Carla heads back downstairs and into the kitchen. Her heart stops, for what feels like a full minute, when she sees her husband. He calmly sips a glass of his favorite white wine at the head of the table.

"A-Albert, what are you doing here?" Carla can barely free the words from her lips.

Albert, Carla's husband is a distinguished older man. He's still incredibly handsome for his age of sixty years old. With his light caramel skin tone, chiseled cheekbones, and those sexy grey specs in his hair, women half his age, especially the ones at his office, throw themselves at him every day.

He used to be a very successful surgeon but has recently taken a position as Vice President of Medical Affairs at St. Luke hospital.

Although he's rich in his own right, there's an air about him that lets you know he comes from money.

"Is there a problem with me having a glass of wine in my own house?" He says, annoyed by the question.

"No, no of course not honey, I just, you just . . ." Carla stammers.

"I know." Albert says cutting her off.

"So, what's for dinner?" He asks leaning back in his chair.

Carla rushes over to the oven and takes out a pan of baked chicken and sets it on top of the stove.

"Um, just some chicken, potatoes, and veggies." Carla says, smiling at Albert as she nervously takes the plates down from the cabinet.

This is the first time Albert has been home for dinner in months. When he is home he'll usually just grabs a plate and takes it upstairs to his bedroom. Lately, Carla has been trying her best to get him to spend more time at home . . . more time with her.

Carla quickly makes a plate and places it in front of him. She grabs the bottle of white wine from the counter and tops off his glass. Her trembling hands causes her to spill a little on the beautiful marble topped dining table.

Albert lets out an aggravated sigh as he rubs his forehead in frustration.

Carla rushes to the sink to grab a dish towel and clean the mess. She pauses with her back toward Albert to collect herself and fight the tears that are ferociously trying to escape her eyes.

She takes a deep breath and heads back to the table.

"I'm so sorry about that sweetie, I don't know where my mind is." She says, as she sops up the wine, her tense smile giving away her embarrassment.

"Just clean it up, it's fine." Albert says in a monotone voice without looking at her.

"So how was your day?" Carla asks as she makes her way back to the stove to fix her plate.

"Fine, I guess." Albert mumbles as he chokes down a mouthful of Carla's famous baked chicken.
"Where's my daughter?" He asks still not looking at her.

"Oh, I don't know what's keeping that girl, she should be down in a minute. How's the chicken?"

"Well, actually, it's a little dry." Albert says giving her a disappointed stare as he spits it out into his napkin.

Albert grabs his plate from the table and makes his way to the trash where he dumps the entire meal in the can, minus the two bites he managed to eat.
Carla looks at him in disbelief as he heads over to the refrigerator and begins to pull out the fixings for a turkey sandwich.

"Oh.... I'm sorry sweetheart; let me do that for you." Carla says, as she jumps up and races to the counter to grab the bread.

She scoots him away from the counter.

"I'll fix it for you dear," she says with an anxious smile.

"Good, I'll be upstairs and could you hurry? I'm starving." He says in a huff as he walks out of the kitchen.

As Albert turns and heads out of the kitchen, Carla feels the tears rise up in her eyes once again. She furiously tries to fight them back to no avail. She gives in and weeps as she slowly spreads Albert's favorite mustard onto a slice of whole wheat bread.

Angela wearily pulls into her driveway. She's been pulling double shifts all week to help pay the bills. Ever since David moved in her expenses have doubled. Despite his promises to get a job, she still finds herself paying all the bills and taking care of him.

Tonight was supposed to be one of the few evenings that she would go out and hang with her girlfriends at their favorite spot. However, putting on her pj's and curling up on the couch, with a glass of her favorite wine, is sounding better right about now. She quickly sends out a text to her friends letting them know she won't be joining them for ladies night.

Angela peels herself out of the car and slowly heads into the house. She kicks off her heels, before making it to the front door, and scoops them into her arms. Her aching feet can't take another step in the gorgeous five inch pumps that perfectly match her blouse.

She walks into the house, tossing her keys and purse on the dining room table, and heads into the kitchen to get started on a quick meal for David. She hurriedly throws together his favorite meatloaf recipe, tosses it in the oven and heads upstairs.

As she drags herself up the stairs she hears the creaking sound of floor boards coming from the second floor of her house. Terrified, Angela runs back downstairs and hides around the corner. She eyes her cell phone on the table but is too afraid to run for it.

David's car wasn't outside so she knows it's not him.

She thinks to herself, "Wait! Jon did say he was coming over to get stuff out of his room this week."

"I bet that's him," she whispers out loud.

She runs upstairs and peeks into Jonathan's room - empty. She hears the creaking floor boards again and realizes exactly where they're coming from . . . her bedroom. She walks slowly across the hall to her bedroom door, takes a deep breath, and gently opens it.

Angela sees a large breasted woman walking around the room setting and lighting candles around her bed. She's completely naked except for a black pair of six inch, thigh high boots. In the corner, a video camera sits atop a tripod and is aimed right at the bed.

"What the hell are you doing?!" Angela screams.

The woman turns and smiles at Angela.

"Oh, hey girl!" She says as if they're old friends. The woman gently sits down on Angela's bed and crosses her legs while still smiling at her.

"Dave went to the store to get some rubbers and beer." The woman says as she giggles.

"He didn't tell me he was bringing a friend tonight. But, umm, you are kind of sexy honey so I guess you can stay." The woman says, biting her finger as she shakes her double D sized breasts at Angela.

"Get the hell out of my house!" Angela screams at the woman, her body shaking with rage.

"Your house? Dave said this was his house . . . Oh! You must be the chick he let stay with him! You're Angie right? The woman stands up and walks over to Angela in an attempt to shake her hand.

"Bitch! You better get the hell out of my house right now before I drag yo' ass out!" Angela screams directly in the woman's face. Noticing the woman's purse and clothes in a chair by the bed, Angela rushes over and begins throwing them at her one at a time.

"Get out!" Angela screams, tears beginning to fall down her face.

"Oh, so he got you thinking you his woman, huh?" she says as she grabs her shirt off of the floor and slips it on.

"Yea, I used to think he was my man too, then I realized his cheating ass ain't never gon' be faithful. So..... I just decided to enjoy him for what he is." The woman slips on a black mini skirt without putting on any underwear.

She walks past Angela and starts to head downstairs. Pausing, she turns and looks at Angela with sincerity in her eyes.

"He's just good sex, honey. That's all he'll ever be."

"Just get the hell out of my house!" Angela screams, her whole body shaking with rage. She collapses onto the floor sobbing uncontrollably.

Fifteen minutes later, David stumbles up the stairs

"Keisha!" Girl, I hope you ready for this . . ." He stops in his tracks when he sees Angela sitting on the bed.

"She's gone, David." Angela says softly.

"The tramp you were about to screw on *MY* bed is gone!"

"Damn! What the hell are you doing home?!" David screams at her as if she betrayed him.
"You said you were going out with your girls tonight."

"What?" You were about to have sex with her in my house! In my bed! And all you can say is what the hell am *I* doing home?" Angela yells.

"Aw, hell, Angie don't start this again!"
"I been honest with you from the start! I told you...."

"You told me you would respect me!" Angela jumps in his face.
"I allowed you to have your whores on the side because I knew you weren't the faithful type. I knew what I was getting into. For some reason, I just always thought that you respected me."

"I do respect you, babe, I love you." David says grabbing her waist.

"No, no you don't." You never did." Angela rips his hands off of her.

"Love shouldn't feel like this, love shouldn't make me feel humiliated . . . stupid . . . disrespected and angry. God, I feel like I'm always angry." Angela says as she slowly sits back down on the bed.

"You know people at work have to remind me to smile every day? I used to smile all the time." Angela whispers sadly.

"So what you want? Huh? You looking for that movie type love. You want the stuff you see on TV? All that crap is fake! What we got is real!" David sits down next to her and puts his arms around her.

"Every relationship has problems."

"I want to be happy, David." Angela says, as she calmly stares at the wall.

"We are happy . . . " He refutes.

"No, you're happy!" And why wouldn't you be? I let you live in my house, I pay all the bills; I buy you food and clothes!"

"Ok, so what about what I do for you?" David screams cutting her off.

"That is exactly my point!" *What do you do for me?*'

"Who washes your car on the weekends, who goes to all your boring office parties with you? Who goes to all them family dinners you don't wanna go to by yourself?" David yells.

Angela slowly stands up and smiles. "Thank you, thank you for reminding me that after all I've done for you, all you can do for me is wash my damn car."

"I want you out of my house by tomorrow."

Angela turns to walk out of the room.

David grabs her hand, walks up close behind her, leans down, and whispers into her ear, "You sure that's what you want?"

Angela freezes, the burst of strength she felt was suddenly beginning to weaken.

David gently caresses her hips and inches closer to her.

"You know I love you Angie. So I'm gon' ask you one more time, are you sure you want me to leave?"

As he whispers, Angela feels his lips gently graze her skin. She feels the warmth of his breath on her neck. Her knees start to go weak. She slowly turns to face him. David grabs her and softly kisses her. Angela tries to fight him but her love for him forces her to surrender to the kiss. She closes her eyes as he pulls her over to the bed.

As she falls on top of him she opens her eyes and sees the video camera the woman setup still standing in the corner. She also notices the candles still surrounding her bed.

Without hesitation, Angela, jumps out of the bed.

"Yes!" She yells . . . "I'm sure."

She takes a final look around the room.

"I'm sure," she whispers to herself, as she heads downstairs.

CHAPTER 2

Jonathan collapses into a chair in the break room of his job at McDonald's. He uses his shirt to wipe the sweat from his brow and rests his head on the table.

"What are you still doing here?" Jonathan's manager walks in, startling him.

"Yea, sorry. I'm leaving, just wanted to rest my eyes for a minute." Jonathan says as he staggers to his feet.

"You've been here all day haven't you?" I wish I was like you when I was your age; young, smart, ambitious. I was all over the place when I was younger."

"Thanks," Jonathan mumbles unenthusiastically as he grabs his jacket and wearily makes his way toward the door.

"Well be careful heading home," The manager says as Jonathan heads out.

"I will, see you tomorrow," Jonathan mumbles.

After his 12 hr shift, Jonathan finally makes his way home. As he pulls up to his apartment he notices Joy's car out front.

"What the hell is she doing here?" Jonathan whispers to himself as he hops out of the car and heads upstairs to his apartment.

As he opens the door he sees Joy sitting on the couch watching TV.

"Finally!" She says as she jumps up and hugs him.

"I've been here for two hours!"

"Babe, I'm kinda tired, I wish you would've called first. Chris let you in?"

Jonathan took in a roommate a few months ago. The bills were piling up and he knew moving back home wasn't an option.

Jonathan likes to joke that Chris has the silver spoon complex. He's never had to work for anything, everything has been handed to him. In fact he can't even get Chris to clean up after himself or shop for groceries. Jonathan is starting to rethink this whole "roommate" thing.

"Yea, he's a nice guy. He told me I could wait here for you. So, what do you want to do tonight?" Joy asks anxiously.

"Babe, I told you, I'm tired." Jonathan says as he sinks down on the couch. "I had class this morning and I worked all day after that."

"I am so sick of you never having time for me! You always have an excuse!" Joy yells.

"Excuse!" Jonathan jumps up to face her. "I work full time and I go to school!

"So you expect me to suffer because you're broke?" Joy yells, but regrets the words as soon as they escape her lips.

Jonathan looks on in disbelief.

He tries to speak but the words won't come quick enough. He always knew that the difference in their backgrounds bothered Joy but it wasn't until that moment that he realized how much.

Joy rushes to his side before he can form a complete thought.

"Babe, I'm sorry. Look, we're both just stressed out and we're saying things we don't mean." Joys explains, as she hugs him. "You know I love you no matter how much money you have. I just want to spend time with you."

"I know." Jon hesitantly agrees, his ego still bruised.

"You still love me?" Joy asks flirtatiously as she kisses his cheek.

"Yea." Jonathan answers reluctantly. "Of course."

Joy eyes Jonathan with those deep cocoa brown eyes that he always seems to get lost in. She flashes him a sly sideways smile. Jonathan, returning her gaze, leans in and kisses her softly.

"Goodnight, I'm going to bed." Jonathan says as he kisses his fiancé on the forehead, his ego is still scarred but he brushes it off.

Although Jonathan has been getting nagging doubts in the pit of his stomach over marrying Joy, he still loves her. She was his first love. Besides, Joy is still pretty upset over the loss of their baby. He can't abandon her now.

"Fine," Joy says still slightly irritated.
"You go get some rest, I'll hang out here for a while just in case you wake up."

Jonathan heads off to his bedroom and closes the door behind him. Joy slumps down on the couch, grabs the remote, and starts flipping through the channels.

Just as she gets lost in reruns and laugh tracks Chris pops out of his room and heads into the living room.

"You still here? I thought you left." Chris smiles as he stands in front of the narrow, full length mirror in the corner of the living

room. He tucks his shirt into his expensive denim jeans.
Chris is what most women would call a "pretty boy". He's the
exact opposite of Jonathan, whose jeans never cost more than
$30.

"Yea, I'm still here. Jon went to bed. Where you goin' looking
all good?" Joy's nostrils flaring as the smell of Chris's cologne
wafts past her nose. Her eyes light up as she watches him slide
his belt on and straighten his pants.

"Me and my boys bout to go see what's poppin' at the club.
What you gettin' into tonight?" Chris asks as he brushes his hair.
His pink lips curl into a smile as he awaits her answer.

"Um, I guess nothing now." I'll probably just head home in a
minute."

"Why don't you call up some of your friends?" he asks as he
slides on his oversized shades and gives himself a final glance in
the mirror.

"I don't have **friends**," Joy says, annoyed by the suggestion.

"Well you look too damn good to be sitting here by yourself on a Friday night." Chris swaggers to the door and opens it.

"Um . . . thanks." Joy blushes, as Chris winks at her and shuts the door.

Carla slowly pulls into the parking lot outside of Albert's office. She checks her makeup in the mirror and grabs a tissue from the dash to blot off the excess lipstick.

"You can do this, Carla," she whispers out loud to herself.

Carla has been trying, with everything inside of her to repair her marriage.

She's grown tired of the silence and the disappointed stares. She wants a real life with Albert. She only wishes they could actually be the couple they pretend to be while they're at those boring parties Albert's colleagues are always throwing.

Today, she's on a mission.

Operation: *Show him what he's been missing* is now underway.

Carla walks into the office and is greeted by Albert's young, perky receptionist. The young woman throws her long blonde hair over her shoulder.

"Can I help you?" she asks with a toothy grin.

"No, I'm just going to talk to my husband." Carla replies, as she heads back to Albert's office.

The blonde hops out of her seat and jumps in front of Carla, stopping her in her tracks.

"Your husband?" She asks as if it's the first time anyone has ever uttered the word. She shakes her head as if erasing the word from her brain.

"Albert doesn't like unannounced guests; you'll have to sit over there until he's ready for you."

"Young lady..." Carla starts.

"Heather." the blonde cuts Carla off.

"Heather, don't you think it's a little inappropriate for you to be calling your boss by his first name? 'Mr. Waters' will do nicely while you're in this office." Carla eyeballs the young girl from head to toe, silently calling her a slut in her mind.

"Actually..." Heather starts, returning Carla's gaze. "He prefers that I call him Albert. Now, you might want to have a seat over there and wait until he's ready for you." Heather's lips curl up into a smile as she gestures for Carla to have a seat.

Carla's nostrils begin to flare as she straightens up her stance and squares off face to face with Heather.

"Young lady, if you value your job, you might wanna sit your ass back down in that seat before . . ."

"Carla!" Albert interrupts. "What are you doing?"

Carla spins around to find Albert staring down at her.

"Oh, Albert. I, um..." Carla stammers.

"What are you doing out here harassing my staff?" Albert walks up to Heather and puts his arm around her.

"Heather are you ok?" He asks looking into her eyes.

"Yea... I'm fine," she answers, haughtily looking back at Carla. She gives Carla a wink and returns to her desk.

Carla grabs Albert by the arm and ushers him back into his office and closes the door behind them.

"Look, sweetie, I didn't come down here to cause trouble. I just wanted to see if I could take my hard working husband out to lunch." Carla says smiling flirtatiously at her husband.

Albert sits on the edge of his desk and folds his arms. "Where the hell do you get off, talking to my staff like that?"

"I'm sorry hun', but she was being extremely rude to me and if she treats me this way I can only imagine how she treats your other visitors." Carla explains.

"I have never had any complaints about . . ." Albert starts.

"Ok, ok . . . I'm sorry. This isn't why I came down here. Look I just want to spend some time with you. You think maybe we could go to lunch and talk?" She steps closer to Albert who's still sitting atop his desk. She runs her hand up his thigh.

"So what do you say?" She smiles.

"My secretary already went to get my lunch, I don't have time for this." Albert tries to move but Carla quickly grabs him and forces him to sit back down.

"Well maybe you don't have time to go out . . ." Carla says as she slowly unbuttons her blouse revealing her bra.
"But maybe you have time for ... other things." her hand slides higher and higher as she leans in and kisses her husband.

It's their first kiss in four months. She reaches for his belt and begins to unbuckle it.

Albert is hypnotized by the sight of his wife's large breasts and the weight of them pressed up against him. He tries to stop Carla's hand from unbuckling his belt but the sensation of her warm tongue gently caressing his neck has him paralyzed.

He tears off his wife's clothes until she stands in his office in only her bra and panties. Albert walks over and locks his office door. Carla slowly makes her way to the couch nestled in the corner of the room; she sits down and slowly crosses her legs, never taking her eyes off of Albert.

Albert walks over to Carla taking off his clothes along the way, his eyes still locked on hers.

He lays her back on the soft plush couch and makes love to his wife for the first time in two years.

Angela, just getting off work, is heading to her car while her mind is still wandering. It has not been a very productive day; she spent the last eight hours trying to get David out of her head. He finally moved out a few days ago. The deafening silence is killing her. She has too much time to think.

As she gets to her car she sees a strange man approaching her quickly out of the corner of her eye. She fumbles to get her keys out of her purse.

"Excuse me, you're Angela right?"

Angela turns to find Will standing there, his dark, cocoa brown skin glistening in the sunlight.

"Yes, you're Will right?" Angela gives him a half smile as she reaches to shake his hand.

Will grabs her hand and pulls her in for a hug.

"Good to see you again," he says as he gives her a firm yet gentle squeeze.

"You too," Angela says as she awkwardly inches back toward her car.

His perfect smile making her blush.

"Where you off to in such a rush?" He asks.

"Just headed home," she says noticing how brown his eyes are.

"Well this is perfect 'cause I was just about to go grab a bite to eat, would you like to join me?"

"Well, um actually I got to um . . ." Angela searches her brain for an excuse but the lie won't come quick enough.

"Aw come on now, you know you gotta eat. Look, there's a place right across the street." Will pleads, as he points to a restaurant across from them.

Angela stares at Will - he's definitely not her usual type. He's dressed a little too nice. She normally goes for men with more of an edge, a little more . . . swag. As he stands there in his khaki pants with his shirt tucked in, Angela notices the kindness in his eyes as he begs her to have dinner with him. Realizing that her normal "type" always leaves her feeling broken and alone she hesitantly agrees.

"Ok," she answers, giving him a nervous smile.

Ten minutes later Angela finds herself sitting across from Will in a quaint Italian restaurant.

"So . . ." she says, leaning forward, resting her elbows on the table, and clasping her hands together beneath her chin.

"What's your story, you got a wife and kids stashed away somewhere?"

Will leans in to match her position.

"Now if I had a wife, would I be here with a lovely woman like you?" He answers confidently.

"Please, don't try that line on me. Cause I know plenty of men who have a gorgeous wife at home and still seem to have time to go to dinner with lovely ladies like myself."

"Oh I see you're just gonna go straight for it huh?" He asks as he chuckles.

"Who has time for games these days," Angela replies, giving him a cocky smile.

"Well, no. I'm not married, never have been. And I don't have any kids either. I always wanted a family but it just never worked out for me." Will's eyes drop to the table but he quickly tries to raise them to mask his hurt.
"I did come close a few times . . ." he continues.

As he goes on about his past, the sincerity in his voice chips away at the wall she's put up to protect her heart.

"So what about you?" He asks, smiling at her with his eyes.

Feeling the need to unload but not wanting to scare him away, She tries not to reveal too much.

"Well I'm actually just coming out of a relationship. I never really required him to stand up and be a man so he never did."

"Well it's not a woman's job to teach a man to be a man. All you can do is show him what you *will* and *won't* tolerate in the relationship." Will interjects.

His response causes a smile to spread across her face.

"Wow." Angela sits back in her chair placing her hands in her lap.

"I've never heard a guy say that before."

"Hey, truth is truth." Will shrugs with a sideways smile.

Angela returns his smile. Their eyes lock for a brief moment. Angela, feeling herself staring, quickly breaks the gaze and grabs her menu.

"So what are you having?" she asks as she thumbs through the pages.

Will notices the swift change of subject. He takes a sip of his water as he debates whether or not to ask his next question. As he places his water on the table, he decides to go for it.

"Did he cheat on you?" Will asks beginning to regret the question when he sees the expression on her face change.

"What?" Angela asks even though she heard exactly what he said.

"Did he cheat on you? Normally when women get cheated on they have a hard time letting their guard down around men. You just seem really guarded and uptight."

Unnerved by his question, Angela sits frozen. Suddenly feeling that all of the hurt, shame and desperation of her past must somehow be plastered all over her face, despite her best efforts to hide it.

"Why would you ask me that?" She asks feeling exposed.

"I'm sorry . . . I didn't mean to offend you. I'm a minister with a background in psychology. Part of my job is reading people, not just listening to their words but hearing their heart. I heard a lot of pain in your voice when you talked about your ex." Will explains, praying he hasn't ruined his chances with her.

"I didn't realize you were a minister." She responds surprised by the revelation.

"Yea, Pastor Johns and I go way back. He asked me to come down and be his assistant Pastor. The church is growing so fast he needs some help to handle all the new people."

"Wow, so you're going to be our new Assistant Pastor?" She asks.

"Well . . . I haven't decided that yet. I told him I'd think about it. I don't know if I want to stay yet. It's a big adjustment going from L.A. to Memphis."

"Well maybe the Lord will give you a reason to stay." Angela blurts out, realizing she's now flirting with a Pastor. Something about him gives her goose bumps, maybe it's his smile or the way his chiseled arms are filling out his white Polo shirt.

"I'm not sure yet, but I think He already has," Will replies as he gives her a crooked smile.

Joy finds herself outside of Jonathan's apartment, again. She knows he isn't home but she couldn't stop herself from showing up early.

As she pulls up she notices Chris' car parked right next to hers.

An inadvertent smile begins to spread onto her face. Over the past few weeks, she and Chris have been playing a sly game of cat and mouse. He flirts with her and she pretends not to notice. Although she must admit that lately her curiosity has been getting the best of her. She can't seem to get him out of her head and as much as she hates to admit it, lately she's been coming over for Chris, not Jonathan.

She sticks her hand in her shirt and adjusts her bra, lifting her breasts to make sure she has just the right amount of cleavage spilling out.

Minutes later she finds herself sitting on the couch with Chris.

"I'm starting to think you like me." He says, with a smirk.

"I can't like you, you're my boyfriend's roommate." She laughs dismissively, hoping he can't see through the lie.

"Ah, ha! So you do you like me!" Chris yells.

"And, why do you assume I like you?"

"Just look at the facts! First of all, you said you can't like me instead of you don't like me. Second, You've been coming over here for weeks claiming that you waiting on Jon, but you always get here at least an hour before he gets off."

"And? That doesn't prove anything," Joy replies, annoyed yet somehow intrigued by his blunt questioning.

"And . . . you blush when I look at you." Chris says, as he slides in closer to her.

Joy looks at him as he stares into her eyes. This is it, she knows he's about to kiss her. She can practically taste his lips as he leans in putting his hand on her thigh.

"Let's watch a movie!" Joy quickly hops up and heads to the DVD stand next to the television. As much as she wants Chris she just can't hurt Jonathan like that.

Chris chuckles to himself as he watches her nervously browse through the DVDs. He slowly walks over to her and gently grazes her hips with the tips of his fingers.

Joy quickly spins around to face him.

"Look, Chris, I can't -"

Before she could finish her thought Chris passionately grabs her and pins her against the wall. He places his hands on her shoulders and slowly moves up her neck. He inches closer to her as he rakes his fingers through her hair.
He leans in and breathes in her perfume as he caresses her lips with his.

CHAPTER 3

Carla slides into a black silk nightgown. She grabs her perfume from the bathroom counter and sprays her neck and wrists. She cracks open the bathroom door and sees that Albert has already slipped into bed.

Over the past two weeks, their bedroom has seen more action than it has throughout their entire marriage. Albert has been coming straight home from work and eating dinner with his family instead of eating alone in his bedroom. Carla couldn't be more pleased, she and Albert finally have the life she always wanted.

She tiptoes over to her husband, pulls the covers back, and slides into bed next to him. Albert slides away from her. Carla moves in again and softly rubs his back.

"Not tonight." Albert rolls over and covers his head with the blanket.

"Are you sure about that?" Carla asks, as she wraps one leg around his waist and kisses his back.

"Damn it, Carla! I said not tonight." Albert rolls over to face her.

Carla sits up in bed.

"What is wrong with you?!" She snaps back at him.

"Look, this isn't working. I'm going to go sleep in the guest room." Albert gets out of bed and heads for the door.

"Honey, wait! We're making progress. Please don't shut down on me again." She pleads with him.

"Sex is not going to fix the problems we have in our marriage. Look, I'm sorry. I thought I could do this, give it another try, work things out, but I can't."

"Why not?" Carla screams at him in frustration.

"I don't trust you! How can I be with someone I can't trust? You lured me into this marriage pretending that you loved me, when all you really wanted was my money. I just can't get over the fact that you never really wanted . . . me."

"Of course I wanted you! What the hell are you talking about?" Carla jumps to her feet.

"No! You wanted this life! You wanted the cars, you wanted the house, and you wanted those expensive ass clothes in your closet! You - never - wanted - me!" Albert's scream echoes throughout their home.

"Albert!" Carla has never heard him raise his voice like this before.

"No! You manipulated me; you knew how much I loved you! I treated you like a queen and all you did was walk all over me for the first ten years of our marriage. I spent ten years begging you to spend time with me. Hell, I had to beg you to have a child with me! I just couldn't understand why it was so hard, and then it finally hit me. You never really loved me. The only reason I stayed was because of Joy."

Carla looks at him and takes a deep breath.

"Ok, I admit it. You're right. Is that what you want to hear? Yes, when we first met, I wasn't that into you. But, Albert, I was a young twenty four year old girl and you were a forty year old man! I thought you were a nice guy who would love me and take care of me. I knew I'd grow to love you eventually and I have.

Albert, honey, I really do love you now."

Carla walks over to him and wraps her arms around him. Albert forces her hands off of him. He stares at her in disbelief.

"Well maybe 'now' is just too damn late." He says fighting the tears in his eyes.

Albert turns to walk out of the bedroom door. He pauses and looks back at his wife with tears in his eyes.

"I loved you from the beginning," he walks out of the room and slowly closes the door behind him.

Angela casually glides into the grocery store. She floats through a sea of housewives rushing past her with screaming toddlers. As they pass she nods and smiles at each one.

She and Will have been dating for three months now and Angela finds herself smiling at everyone lately.

This man is amazing. He has literally kissed away every tear and made her feel like a woman again. He loved her past her pain and shows her, everyday, how a real man should treat a woman.

Angela pulls her shopping list out of her purse. Tonight she's cooking dinner for Will. As she peruses the isles, she hears a strangely familiar laugh coming from the next isle.

It stops her in her tracks.

"Now, I know that's not who I think it is." She whispers to herself.

Curiosity overtakes her and forces her to rush around the corner and peek into the aisle. Her heart jumps into her throat when she sees David standing there . . . and he's not alone.

Angela hides herself next to a tall display of salad dressing; her heart pounding so loud it seems everyone in the store can hear it. She tries to calm herself as she peeks around the display.

The woman is absolutely gorgeous. She bends over in her skin tight jeans, to fix the clasp on her plat-formed, high heeled shoe. The woman notices him staring at her. She leans in and kisses David's cheek and smiles at him. He slaps her on the butt and she playfully pushes him away. He grabs her and pulls her into his chest. The pair shares a long and passionate kiss.

"Oh I don't believe this." Angela says, unable to take her eyes off of them.

"She can't be more than twenty five years old!"

Suddenly Angela notices David looking in her direction. She tries to duck back behind the salad dressing but it's too late. She's been spotted.

"Angie? Angie is that you?" David quickly makes his way over to her with the woman scampering behind him.

"Oh, hey! Yea, I thought that was you." She exclaims trying to mask her humiliation.

David rushes in and gives her a tight hug. She smells his cologne. That intoxicating musk fills her mind with old memories, both good and bad.

"Wow, talk about a small world." David mumbles awkwardly. His date pushes past him.

"Hi, I'm Nichole." She says boldly, reaching out to shake Angela's hand.

"Nice to meet you, I'm Angela." Angela finds herself in a trance as she stares at the woman's long beautiful hair and huge perky breasts.

Realizing this is getting awkward she quickly blurts out, "So how do you two know each other?"

"Well we've been dating for a while now." He says grabbing Nichole's hand.

"And now we're engaged!" Nichole happily chimes in and holds up her hand; revealing a white gold, solitaire ring, at least 2 carats.

Angela feels the rage bubbling up inside her. Everything suddenly has a reddish glow.

"En-engaged?" She forces the word out of her mouth.

She feels her heart fall out of her chest and splatter down on her shoes. Her eyes are locked on David, waiting for him to say something, anything to make this untrue.

She screams at him in her mind to say something. "Say something!" she yells inside herself. "Call this young bitch a liar and shove her across the room! Say, something!" Her mind yells.

David puts his arm around Nichole's waist and pulls her closer to him.

"Yea, we're getting married in six months."

"Babe, I'll let you catch up with your friend and I'll run and get the rest of the food. Nice to meet you, Angela." She gives him two quick pecks on the lips.

Each one drives a bullet through Angela's heart.

As Nichole scurries away, Angela still finds herself frozen, unable to speak. She finally squeaks out the only thing she can think of in that moment.

"Engaged?"

"Yea, I'm finally doing it. Never thought I'd ever be getting married." He shakes his head in disbelief.

"Well, that makes two of us." Angela agrees. "I thought you said you never wanted to get married."

"Well I guess when you find the right woman, anything is possible." David gives her a cocky grin.

"I guess so. Well, I'm glad you're happy - congratulations." Angela says with her last ounce of courage.
She turns and heads in the opposite direction, praying that she can make it out of the store before the tears come.

Joy sits in the cold brightly lit office of her family physician, Dr. Karen White. She's been taking care of Joy and her family for as long as Joy can remember.

"Hey Joy!" Dr. Karen says, as she rushes into her office. "I'm so sorry I couldn't treat you myself but I've been absolutely swamped this week. I hope my nurse took good care of you. She told me you think you might have the flu." She says as she flips through the results of Joys' tests.

"Yes, there has to be some sort of bug going around . . " Joy starts. "I've just been feeling awful lately. I'm always hot and nauseous. My energy is completely drained. I've even thrown up a few times."

Dr. Karen's eyes lock on one line on the chart. The smile she had been wearing suddenly fades. She slowly looks up at Joy. Joy notices the concern on her favorite doctor's face.

"What's wrong? Am I sick, i-is it serious? Joy sits on the edge of her seat.

Dr. Karen slides her glasses off, neatly folds them and slowly places them on her desk.

"Baby girl . . . this is very serious. Joy . . . you're pregnant."

Joy feels as if all of the air has been sucked out of the room. She gasps as if taking her last breath.

"Pregnant . . . I-I can't be pregnant." She says, holding on to her chair.

"Joy, the nurse gave you a urine test and a blood test. They both came out positive. Now honey, I'm just as shocked as you are but believe me, you're pregnant." Dr Karen explains.

"How did this happen to me?" Joy asks out loud to herself.

"Well, sweetie, you tend to get pregnant . . . when you have sex." Dr. Karen gives Joy a smirk. Ever since Joy was a little girl, she's always been able to make her laugh, whether she was setting a broken bone or giving a shot.

"Stop it, Karen, this isn't funny!" Joy snaps.

"Oh calm down, girl! Ladies your age get pregnant every day, it's not the end of the world. Besides, Jonathan is good guy; he'll be there for you."

Joy tightens her grip on her chair.

"Oh my god." She says under her breath, as she thinks back to her night with Chris.

"Yea . . . he's gonna make a great father." Joy says, as a single tear rolls down her cheek.

An hour later Joy finds herself once again sitting in her car outside of Jonathan's apartment. He finally managed to get an off day and invited her over for lunch.

Joy tries to fix her makeup in the rearview mirror but the tears keep coming. Who knows if Jonathan would have forgiven her for cheating on him, but now that she's pregnant by Chris she fears that once he finds out, their relationship is over.

She collects herself and heads inside of Jon's apartment.

"Hey babe!" Jon shouts as he rushes to greet her.
"Look I'm sorry I've been so busy lately. I was thinking about it and you're right. I need to be spending more time with you." Jon pulls out a chair at the dining room table.
"So sit down, today is all about me and you." He leans in and kisses her cheek.

Page | 55

Joy sits at the table unable to gather her thoughts. She wants to come clean about the cheating and the pregnancy but the words won't come.

At that moment Chris walks in and sits across from Joy.

"What's up miss lady?" He says, with a flirtatious grin.

"Aww babe I'm sorry. I told Chris he could join us for lunch. You don't mind do you?" Jon asks, poking his head out of the kitchen.

"Um . . . no, its fine." She agrees hesitantly.
"Hi," she says almost embarrassed to look at Chris.

Chris reaches out and grabs her hand lying on the table. She instantly snatches it from him.

"Why you trippin'?" he asks, whispering so Jonathan doesn't hear him.

"Just stop," she says, giving him a stern look.

At that moment, Jonathan pops out of the kitchen.

"Damn, I forgot something! I'm gonna run to the store." Jonathan goes to grab his keys.

"No, babe, don't leave. Whatever it is, it's not that important."

"Yes it is, I'll be back in twenty minutes. Y'all just relax; the lasagna needs another half hour anyway."

Jonathan grabs his keys and wallet and runs out of the front door.

As soon as he hears the lock turnover on the door, Chris starts moving towards Joy.

Joy jumps up from her seat and heads into the living room to avoid him.

"Aw don't try to run, girl," Chris laughs, still following her.

"Look, I can't do this anymore. What happened between us was a mistake. I love Jonathan." Joy explains, suddenly feeling as if someone turned the heat on too high and she might throw up. She wipes sweat from her brow.

Noticing the ill expression on her face Chris moves in close to her.

"Are you ok?" He asks.

Joy pushes past him and races to the bathroom where she falls to her knees and vomits in the toilet.
Chris helps Joy to her feet and grabs a towel, quickly dampens it, and wipes her face clean. He wraps his arms around her as she sobs on his shoulder.

"Look, I'm sorry for messing around earlier. I didn't know you were sick."
He says as he sweeps her hair away from her face.

"I'm not sick. I think I had some bad eggs for breakfast. I'm fine." She says, spinning away from him. She turns toward the mirror and checks her makeup, then grabs the mouthwash, sitting on the counter, and swishes it around her mouth before spitting it in the sink.

As she turns to walk out of the bathroom, she suddenly begins to feel as if she might throw up again. She puts her hand over her mouth as she dry heaves.

"Are you pregnant?" Chris asks with a shocked yet concerned expression.

"Pregnant? No, I told you, it's something I ate. I'll be fine." Joy steadies herself against the towel rack.
"I just need to get out of this bathroom, it's filthy in here! Do y'all ever clean up?" She says throwing a dirty towel at him.

"No, you've been acting weird since you got here. You're pregnant!" Chris yells, following her as she stomps out of the bathroom.

"Ok! Damn, Sherlock! Yes, I'm pregnant, now will you shut the hell up?" Joy shrieks at him.

"Jon doesn't know yet."

"Aw man, he is gonna freak out!" Chris laughs. He stops abruptly when he notices the awkwardness of Joys' expression.

"You don't think it's mine, do you?" He asks curiously.

"Honestly, I don't know." Joy explains as she sits slowly on the couch.
"I mean, one night I'm with him, the next night I'm with you."

"I just feel so stupid! This stuff just doesn't happen to girls like me. This crap happens to hood chicks named Bonquisha! This does not happen to me!" Joy cries.

"I can't believe I'm sitting here trying figure out who my baby daddy is! This is so embarrassing!"

"Well I want a blood test." Chris interrupts her rant.

"What?" Joy asks, snapping back to the reality of the situation.

"When the baby is born, I want a blood test. I need to know if it's mine. I just can't have some other man out there raising my child." Chris says sternly.

"How very noble of you, but are you insane?" Joy laughs. "I don't care whose child it is, as far we're all concerned, Jonathan is the father! He can't know anything about this!"

"Look, you are not just gonna take my child from -" Chris starts but is interrupted by the sound of Jonathan's keys in the door.

Jonathan opens the door and walks in with a dozen pink roses, Joys' favorite.

"Aww baby! They're beautiful!" Joy flies off the couch and gives him a tight hug.

"Well I meant to get them earlier but it slipped my mind. I'm sorry."

"Thanks babe, I love you." She says looking in his eyes.

"I love you too." Jon gives her a soft kiss on her forehead.

Chris watches as the pair head off into the kitchen, hand in hand. Infuriated, he rages out of the front door slamming it behind him.

CHAPTER 4

Carla finds herself in the middle of another party filled with Albert's colleagues.

The tension between them is mounting with each passing day, but as always, they keep up appearances.

As they glide through the room arm in arm smiling and rubbing elbows with other wealthy Memphians, Carla's smile begins to crack. She can't smile through one more party pretending to be happily married. She has to get out.

"Excuse me for a moment," she says politely, as she gently kisses Albert's cheek. She drops his hand and moves as quickly as she can toward the door.

As she makes her way through a maze of socialites she finally finds freedom on the balcony overlooking a breathtaking view of the Mississippi river. Just as the breeze of the night air begins to soothe her mind, she hears the balcony doors open. Unable to bear the thought of another boring conversation punctuated with fake smiles and even faker laughter, she ducks behind a pillar against the side of the house.

"I've been waiting to get you alone all night," Albert moans, as he corners Heather against the railing of the balcony.

"I cannot believe he invited her here!" Carla whispers to herself as she peeks around the corner.

"Not so fast." Heather says, as she pushes Albert off of her. "Why would you invite me **and your wife** to the same party? I never would have come here if I knew she'd be here! I'm humiliated! I can only imagine how she must feel."

"Look, I invited you here because I'm tired of hiding you.

We're in love, we should be together and I never invited her . . .

she just assumed she should come. I guess I didn't have the

nerve to tell her I didn't want her here." Albert explains.

"I don't even know why I'm involved with you. I'm not the

type of woman who sleeps around with married men. What

happened to all those promises you made about leaving your

wife?" Heather asks with one hand on her hip.

"Well, I went to see a lawyer last week. The papers are

already drawn up and on my desk." Albert grabs Heather and

pulls her close to him. "I can't take this anymore - I'm asking her

to sign them tomorrow."

The two of them share a passionate kiss.

Carla feels her heart sink into her stomach. She stares down at

her gorgeous 5 carat diamond wedding ring. Suddenly her

sadness turns into rage.

Angela finds herself sitting in front of the fireplace at Will's

cozy apartment.

"I think I've made my decision, I'm staying in Memphis." He says with a smile.

Ever since Angela ran into David at the grocery store, she can't get him out of her mind. This is made worse by the fact that he recently started texting her begging to see her again.

"Wow, that's amazing!" She says as he leans in and gives her a kiss.

She's fallen in love with Will over the past few months. No man has ever treated her the way he does. She feels a glow surrounding them whenever they're together. Will is the exact opposite of David. He's unafraid to proclaim his love whenever he sees her. He gives her all of the love and affection she's been desperately craving.

However, there is one issue.

Will is celibate and has decided not to have sex until he's married. Angela on the other hand has been having sex regularly since she was sixteen. The stress of celibacy is starting to get to her.

"You look beautiful tonight," Will says as he strokes her hair and gazes into her eyes. "You know, I thank God for you every day? I love you so much." He says, smiling at her.

"I love you too." She says as she slides in closer to him. She places her hand on his knee and slowly moves up his thigh.

Will quickly grabs her hand and pulls it up to his mouth and gives it soft kiss.

"Slow down, babe. We got the rest of our lives for that. Let's just enjoy this moment." He jumps to his feet.

"I'll get us some wine." He says, as he turns and heads to the kitchen.

Angela collapses onto the couch and blankly stares into the fire. She can't imagine how she can be so in love with a man she's never slept with.

The beep of her cell phone snaps her out of her trance. Its David . . . again.

"I need to see you tonight."

She stares at the phone feeling the heat start to rise in her body.

She feels as if she's torn between two halves of herself. She can either stay here with the man who takes care of her heart or go find the man who has always taken care of her body.

As if making the decision for her, her thumb quickly types out a simple reply:

"Where?"

"I have to go," she calls into the kitchen. She jumps off of the couch, quickly slides her feet into her shoes and grabs her purse off of the chair by the door.

"What? Where you going?" Will shouts as he pokes his head out of the kitchen.

"I'm sorry, I just gotta get out of here," she says as she runs out and closes the door behind her.

Will stares at the door as if he knows she is going to walk back in at any second.

Once he realizes that she's not coming back he slowly sits down on his couch.

He reaches into his pocket and pulls out a small black box and places it neatly on the coffee table.

The next morning Angela lies awake in her bedroom staring at the ceiling, to her left David lies sleeping peacefully.

The sight of him brings tears to her eyes.

Her anger bubbles up inside of her forcing her to punch him repeatedly until he wakes up.

"I hate you!" She screams still swinging at him as he ducks and tries to grab her arms.

"What the hell is wrong with you now?!" He yells, as he pins her arms down.

"You have screwed up my entire life!" she screams, as she struggles to free herself from his grip.

"Why do you do this every time?" He yells, as he shoves her far enough away that she can't reach him.

"You have had this hold on me since I was sixteen, every time I'm around you I turn into that same little girl. I don't know what is wrong with me." She says, as she finally calms down.

"Why the hell are you swinging at me?" He screams while putting on his clothes.

"You a grown ass woman, I can't make you do nothing you don't wanna do." He says smirking as he zips his pants.

"No, you know exactly what you're doing. You manipulate me every chance you get and I'm tired of it!" Angela yells as David walks towards the door.

David stops, looks at her and laughs to himself.

"Look, you can try to blame me all you want, but you and I both know what happened. You were horny and you needed to get some." He walks over to her and puts his arm around her shoulder.

"Ay, I'm fine with this arrangement. We can do this as long as you need to. I know it's not easy for you being wit' a man that ain't givin' you none. How bout you just call me next time you need . . . a friend." David kisses her cheek and heads out of the house.

Angela grabs a pillow from her bed and flings it at him right as the door closes. She can't figure out whether it was his arrogance that pissed her off or if it was the fact that his offer intrigued her.

Joy stares at Jonathan from across the table at their favorite restaurant. Its Jonathan's birthday and Joy wanted to treat her man to dinner. Besides, she figures it'll be the perfect time to break the news about the baby.

"Happy birthday sweetie," Joy smiles, as she slides a blue box with gold ribbon across the table to Jon.

"Thanks, babe." Jon says as he grabs the box and rips off the paper.

"You know I didn't want you to buy me anything."

"Well, technically I didn't." Joy smirks, as he lifts the lid off of the box.

As soon as he peers inside of the box Jonathan freezes, his smile begins to fade. He slowly reaches inside and pulls out a small black and white sonogram.
Jonathan sits there speechless as he stares at it.

"Jon, honey, say something." Joy insists, feeling as if he can tell from the pea sized fetus that it's not his baby.

"You're . . . pregnant?" Jon asks in disbelief. He's still unable to take his eyes off of the picture.

"Yea, I am" Joy replies, staring down at the table.
"I was afraid to tell you, I didn't know how you'd feel about it after what happened last time."

Jonathan is still staring at the sonogram unable to speak. Joy notices the tears fill his eyes.

"I guess I'm just in shock," Jonathan finally begins to speak. "I watched you go through so much pain last time." A single tear rolls down his cheek.

"You and everybody were just so upset and I never cried with y'all. I wanted to be strong . . . I wanted to be strong for you." Jonathan's fists clenched as more tears stream down his face.

"I just remember being so . . . angry. I used to cry every night." Jon says as he aggressively swats the tears from his face.

Joy feels her heart crack in two as she watches the love of her life break down.

"Why were you angry?" She asks wiping away her own tears.

"I wanted that baby. I wanted to show my father . . . this is how you raise a child!" Jon says angrily.
"I wanted to show his ass that it can be done! Here! This is how you do it! Let me be yo' example since yo' ass sho' as hell couldn't teach me!" Jon puts his hands over his face as he sobs.

Joy hops up and rushes to the opposite side of the booth where Jon is sitting. She slides in next to him and wraps her arms around him as he cries.
Jonathan reaches down and places his hand on her stomach.

"I hope it's a boy," he says, as a slight smile spreads across his tear soaked face.

"Me too." Joy replies softly, as she places her hand on top of his.

Angela sneaks into the church on a Wednesday night. She sits in the far corner near the door as she watches Will giving his closing remarks for tonight's bible study.

It's been three days since she ran out of his apartment and the two haven't spoken since.

She was too embarrassed to call or text; besides, she figures she owes him an explanation, face to face.

After he gives the closing prayer, he and the other parishioners head out into the lobby of the church. Some say their goodbyes and head out to their vehicles as others huddle together discussing tonight's lesson.

"Will!" Angela shouts as she rushes to catch him before he gets to his car.

Will stops at his car door and turns to see Angela rushing across the parking lot.

"I gotta say you are the last person I expected to see here tonight," he says, as she catches up to him.

"Well, I felt like we needed to talk." Angela says as her eyes drop to her shoes.

"I think you made yourself pretty clear when you ran out of my house that night." Will says in a low whisper as he smiles and waves at one of the church goers passing by.

"I'm sorry" Angela pleads. "I love you but this is hard for me."

"What's hard for you? The way I listen to you, the way I make sure you're taken care of emotionally? I know you've been hurt. Baby, I'm trying to love you past your pain, past your fears." Will looks her in the eyes. "Exactly what is so hard about that for you?"

"And I love you for that!" Angela chimes in. "I'm just not used to it. I've been having sex since I was sixteen. I feel so stupid for saying this, but that's how I could tell if a guy was interested in me, you know? If he tried to sleep with me. I guess part of me didn't feel like I was worthy of a man like you."

"That's because you're wounded, right here." He places his hand on her heart.
"You don't believe you're worthy of a man . . . who just wants *you*." Will places his hands on her face and wipes the tears that are slowly beginning to fall.

"We got the rest of our lives for sex. I'm trying to connect with your spirit. Are you ready for that?"

"Yea, I'm ready . . . but I wanna tell you something before we move forward. I want to be honest with you." Angela says, as she begins nervously wringing her hands.
"It's about where I went when I left your house that night."

"Stop." Will grabs her shoulders and looks in her eyes. "You don't have to say anymore."

"But I want to be completely......"

"Just stop!" Will insists. "I already know. You went to see David didn't you? Angela slowly nods her head, yes.

"Is it over, are you done with him?" Will asks sternly.

Angela ponders the question in her mind. Can she ever really be done with the man she's loved since she was a girl? Can she ever truly walk away and never see him again?

Angela quickly blurts out what she knows he wants to hear.

"Yes, It's over!" She's says as she grabs Will and squeezes him tightly.

"I hope so," she says silently to herself.

It's been a week since Carla overheard Albert plotting the end of their marriage with Heather. Ever since then she's been avoiding him. There is no way she's just gonna lie back and let it happen.

Albert called to say he'd be home soon and asked her to stay put so they could "talk".

"I guess this is it." She says to herself, as she hangs up her cell phone.

Carla tosses her phone on the table and runs around the house collecting all of Albert's Epi Pens. Albert has severe allergies and keeps the pens in almost every room in the house. She dumps all of the pens in her purse and rushes back to the kitchen to grab the last pen out of the drawer by the sink. She shoves it in her pocket and rushes back to the stove to finish preparing Albert's favorite, Cornish Hen with cranberry stuffing. However tonight she'll serve it with a new ingredient, walnuts.

Ever since the day they met, Albert has warned her about serving him anything with nuts in it. In fact, he has forbid her from keeping nuts in the house. A single tear flows down her face as she grinds the nuts into Albert's favorite stuffing.

An hour later, Carla sets the plates at the kitchen table. She pulls out their best crystal stemware and pours his favorite white wine in the glasses.

As if on cue Albert walks in.

"Hey sweetie, welcome home." Carla says as she sits at the table casually sipping her wine.

"Hello," he says, as he looks around the kitchen.

"Look, I'm glad you're here, we have some things we need to discuss." He says noticing that his favorite meal is on the stove.

"I know we do, we have a lot of issues we need to resolve. But tonight, I just wanted to cook for you. You always did love my cooking right?" She walks over to him and helps him take off his jacket.

"Yes, but we still need to talk." Albert answers.

"Fine, we can talk over dinner." Carla insists as she ushers him over to a chair at the table.

She sits across from him and watches as he slowly begins shoveling the food into his mouth.

"So what did you want to talk about?" She digs, knowing full well what's coming.

Albert's already eaten half of his stuffing before he comes up for air.

He takes a sip of wine and cautiously begins to speak.

"I really don't know how to say this," he starts.

"Say what?" Carla leans in, setting her wine on the table.

"I'm just not happy, and know you're not either." he explains as he loosens his tie and wipes sweat from his forehead.

"What makes you think I'm not happy?" Carla asks, noticing Albert beginning to scratch his hands and throat.

"Don't play games with me, Carla!" Albert says as more sweat forms on his brow.

"This marriage has run its course, I want a di -" Albert starts coughing uncontrollably as he fights to gasp for air. He's suddenly finding it increasingly hard to swallow.

"What's wrong honey?" Carla asks as an arrogant grin spreads across her face.

Still gasping for air as his throat slowly tightens, Albert hops up from the table and rushes to the drawer near the sink. He shovels all of its contents onto the floor as he feverishly searches for his Epi pen.

Collapsing onto the floor, he crawls toward the kitchen door trying to get to the hall bathroom; he knows there's another pen in the top drawer.

"Now what's that you were saying honey? You want a di-divorce?" Carla let's out an explosive laugh as she watches Albert gasp for air.

"You want me to slink away with my tail between my legs while you marry your little blonde haired, blue eyed bitch!" She screams as she sweeps her plate off of the table. It crashes against the wall with shards of glass spreading across the floor.

Carla walks out of the room leaving Albert wheezing on the floor. She returns a few seconds later holding a manila folder. She slams it on the floor next to a still suffering Albert.

"So, YOU decided that YOU were done with OUR marriage!"

She says as she sits next to Albert on the floor.

Albert grabs at her expensive Prada blouse. He's unable to speak but his eyes say everything he can't.

Carla rips his hands off of her.

"Well I'm a realist, I understand that these things don't always work out" she says blankly staring at the wall.

"However, if you want to leave, I have a few . . . demands." Carla says as she snaps out of her trance.

"You remember that ugly little prenuptial agreement you forced me to sign when we got married, don't you darling?" She says opening the folder and sliding it in front of his face.

"Well I had some papers drawn up myself; these documents will dissolve our pre-nup." She places a pen in his hand.

"But don't worry; I won't leave you completely destitute. I only want half... of everything." Carla smiles at her husband. "Oh, I'm also keeping the house. I'm sure you'll be able to arrange some other place to live, darling. Perhaps Heather has an extra bedroom."

Albert shakes his head and throws the pen at Carla.

"I was afraid you'd feel that way, sweetie." Carla reaches into her pocket and pulls out the Epi Pen.

Albert lunges at her with his last ounce of strength; he misses and lands with his face planted on Carla's papers.

Albert's wheezing slows as his throat closes tighter and tighter.

"Last chance, darling." Carla's smile turns into a vicious scowl. "Sign the damn papers!" She screams, putting the pen in his right hand. She curls his fingers around it and steadies his hand on the paper. A single tear drop splashes on the paper as Albert tightens his grip and scribbles his signature. He collapses with his face on the papers and closes his eyes as if embracing his impending death.

Carla uncaps the Epi Pen and leans over her husband. She can still hear a faint wheezing coming from his lifeless body. She rolls him over on his back, unbuttons his pants and pulls them down around his knees. She quickly jabs the Epi Pen in his right thigh and holds it there for a few seconds before yanking it out and throwing it across the room.

She sits next to Albert and weeps uncontrollably as she thinks of her marriage. She's startled out of her recall by Albert taking his first full breath. She leans over him and gently kisses his forehead. She grabs the papers under his head and runs out of the room.

Stay tuned for the next part of the Joy series!

Miss part one? Want more of Joy? Visit Kimberly Kirby's website! www.KimJKirby.com

About the Author

Kimberly Kirby is an American author who resides in Memphis, TN. She writes poetry, children's books, songs, and scripts for the silver screen. Kimberly is also the author of *What to Do Until He Finds You* and the *Joy series*.

Angela, alone in her house, sits quietly in the corner of her bedroom. She grabs a pen and paper from the nightstand. After a minute of false starts, she begins to write:

What is this?

This, that forces me to be weak. Forces me to allow you to walk all over me and yet I grin, and knowingly bear it.

What is this?

This, that rips my identity from my hands and causes me to willingly give it over to you with hardly a second thought.

What is this?

This, that comforts me as your deceit tears through my self esteem.

What is this?

This, that with overwhelming assurance allows me to lie still as you use and abuse my body and my virtue.

What is this?

This, that takes my strength, strength that once birthed nations and turns it into helplessness.

Your name, I'm told, is loneliness.

www.ingramcontent.com/pod-product-compliance
Lightning Source LLC
Chambersburg PA
CBHW070531130626
46555CB00003B/1361